To Evan and Lulu, with love
—R. B.

To Vicki Morgan and Gail Gaynin
—B. G.

NOTE FROM THE ILLUSTRATOR:
I sketch ideas for each illustration with pen and
paper. I use the memory of these preliminary
hand-drawn pieces when I go to the computer to
create the final illustrations. I start by exploring
color on-screen to find the perfect tones to embody
what I want to say in my art. I draw and paint with
a digital pen on a tablet and then layer the solid
colors with textures to bring the illustrations to life.
—B. G.

SIMON & SCHUSTER BOOKS FOR YOUNG READERS • An imprint of
Simon & Schuster Children's Publishing Division • 1230 Avenue of the
Americas, New York, New York 10020 • Text copyright © 2009 by Robert
Burleigh • Illustrations copyright © 2009 by Beppe Giacobbe • All rights
reserved, including the right of reproduction in whole or in part in any form. • SIMON
& SCHUSTER BOOKS FOR YOUNG READERS is a trademark of Simon & Schuster, Inc. • Book
design by Chloë Foglia • The text for this book is set in Geometrica 415. • The cover
type and typography in artwork are all hand-lettered. • Manufactured in China •
10 9 8 7 6 5 4 3 2 1

Library of Congress Cataloging-in-Publication Data • Burleigh, Robert. • Clang! Clang!
Beep! Beep! : listen to the city / Robert Burleigh ; illustrated by Beppe Giacobbe.—1st
ed. • p. cm. • "A Paula Wiseman book." • Summary: From morning until night, a city is
filled with such sounds as the roars and snores of a subway ride, the flutters and coos
of pigeons, and the shouts and beeps of drivers in traffic. • ISBN: 978-1-4169-4052-4
(hardcover : alk. paper) • [1. Stories in rhyme. 2. Noise—Fiction. 3. Sound—Fiction.
4. City and town life—Fiction.] I. Giacobbe, Beppe, ill. II. Title. • PZ8.3.B9526Clg 2009 •
[E]—dc22 • 2007045844

CLANG! CLANG! BEEP! BEEP!

LISTEN TO THE CITY

BY ROBERT BURLEIGH

ILLUSTRATED BY BEPPE GIACOBBE

A Paula Wiseman Book

Simon & Schuster Books for Young Readers

New York   London   Toronto   Sydney

Alarm clock ringing,
Eardrums stinging . . .

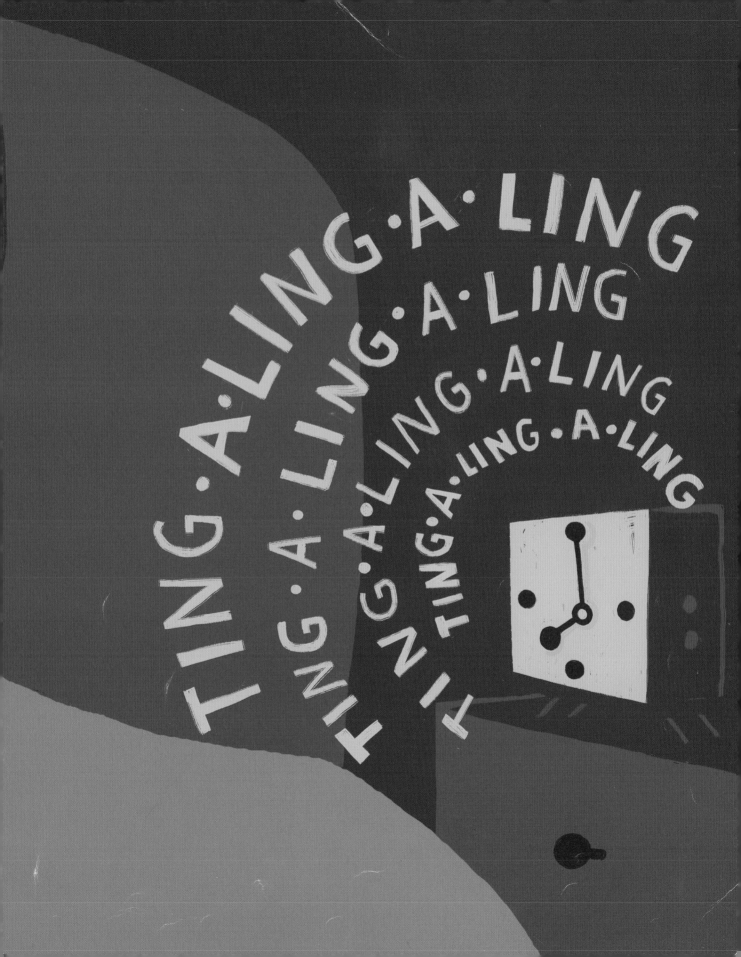

THUNK
THUNK
CLUNK!

Big truck rocking,
Trash cans knocking.

Subway roaring,
Riders snoring.

FLUTTER FLUTTER

**Pigeons strutting,
Kids shortcutting.**

Bridge arms lifting,
Barges drifting.

Sidewalk chalking,
Jump rope talking.

RING RING RING RING

RING RING

**Big crowd yelling,
Ice cream selling.**

WOO!

OH·EE

**Traffic streaming,
Siren screaming.**

Drivers shouting,
In-and-outing.

Wrecking ball smashing,
High wall crashing.

**Red sun sinking,
Streetlights blinking.**

**Moonlight beaming,
Children dreaming.**

SHHHHH!

SHHHHH!

Darkness creeping,
City sleeping. . . .